This book is a work of fiction. Any references to historical events, real people, or real places are used fictitiously. Other names, characters, places, and events are products of the author's imagination, and any resemblance to actual events or places or persons, living or dead, is entirely coincidental.

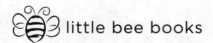 little bee books

An imprint of Bonnier Publishing USA
251 Park Avenue South, New York, NY 10010
Copyright © 2017 by Bonnier Publishing USA
All rights reserved, including the right of reproduction
in whole or in part in any form.
LITTLE BEE BOOKS is a registered trademark of Bonnier Publishing USA,
and associated colophon is a trademark of Bonnier Publishing USA.
Manufactured in the United States of America BVG 0317
ISBN: 978-1-4998-0644-1
First Edition 10 9 8 7 6 5 4 3 2 1

littlebeebooks.com
bonnierpublishingusa.com

Tales of
SASHA

3 Books in 1!

little bee books

Tales of
SASHA

The Big Secret

by Alexa Pearl

illustrated by Paco Sordo

Contents

Go! Go! Go!

"Sasha! Come back!"

Sasha's ears perked up, but she did not stop running. She was having too much fun. She ran past her friends. She ran past her two sisters. Faster and faster. The wind flowed through her glossy mane. The sun felt warm on her back. The spring grass was bright green beneath her hooves.

Up ahead, she spotted the stream. She did not slow down. She ran toward it.

One . . . two . . . three! Sasha counted to herself. Then she leaped into the air. Her body felt so light it was like she was floating in the clouds. *This is the best feeling EVER!* she thought.

Sasha landed on the
other side of the stream.
A forest of tall trees
stood in front of her.

"Sasha! Come back!"

Her mom's voice stopped her. Sasha knew that tone. That tone meant her mom was upset, and Sasha knew why. The horses in their valley all had the same rule: Never go beyond the big trees.

Now she was standing in front of the big trees. She had never run this far before.

What is beyond the trees? she wondered.

No one in Verdant Valley knew. Not Mom. Not Dad. Not her teacher. Not her sisters.

I hate not knowing things, Sasha thought. *Someday I will go there. Someday I will find out.*

Sasha splashed back through the stream. She trotted to her family.

Her mom frowned. "I warned you not to run too far, Sasha," she said.

"I'm sorry," said Sasha.

Mom nuzzled her with her nose. Sasha nuzzled back. Sasha's mom never stayed angry with her.

"Was someone chasing you?" asked her sister Zara. Zara was the oldest sister in their family. Poppy was in the middle, and Sasha was the youngest.

Sasha laughed. "No. Why?"

"You were running so fast," said Zara.

"Running makes me tired and sweaty," said Poppy.

Running makes me super happy, Sasha thought.

She had once tried to tell her sisters about how great she felt when she ran. They did not understand. They liked to spend their days eating grass and talking. Sasha thought that was boring.

Zara and Poppy were so different from Sasha. They looked different too.

Zara was jet-black with a chestnut brown mane and tail. Poppy was chestnut brown with a jet-black mane and tail. Their dad called them the "flip-flop sisters." Everyone could see that they belonged together.

And then there was Sasha. She was pale gray—except for a small white patch on her back. Her tail and mane were gray too. *Borrrring!* thought Sasha.

Whenever she ran, Sasha pretended that she was shiny silver. She pretended that her mane glittered. She even pretended that rainbow sparkles exploded from her tail.

Sasha wished she looked as sparkly as she felt. She wished she could be a "flip-flop sister" too.

"I'm putting flowers in Zara's mane," said Poppy.

"Do you want flowers in yours?" asked Zara.

"Yes!" said Sasha. "We can *all* wear pretty flowers."

Poppy tucked a flower into Sasha's mane, but it fell out. Poppy put in another flower, but that one fell out too.

"Sasha!" cried Poppy. "Stay still. The flowers are falling."

I stink at staying still, thought Sasha, but she tried to be like her sisters. She tried not to move. Then her hooves did a little dance. Her body wanted to go, go, go!

Wyatt trotted over. Wyatt was Sasha's better-than-best friend. He swatted her with his tail.

"Tag! You're it!" cried Wyatt.

Sasha was off! She chased after Wyatt. All the flowers fell out, but Sasha did not care.

Wyatt was fast, but Sasha was faster!

CHAPTER 2

Head in the Clouds

"Got you!" Sasha tagged Wyatt.

"Let's play again," said Wyatt. "This time you won't catch me."

"Sure!" But Sasha knew she would catch him. She always did.

A loud whinny echoed through the valley. The whinny sounded again. Caleb, their teacher, was calling them.

"It's time for school," said Wyatt.

Caleb waited in the shade of a pine tree. All the young horses trotted over to him. Zara and Poppy galloped up. Sasha and Wyatt went too.

Caleb was the oldest horse in their valley. There were flecks of gray in his copper coat. He had taught Sasha's parents when they were young. Caleb was very smart. He knew everything about everything.

"Today, we will learn to walk in a line." Caleb spoke very slowly.

"But why?" asked Twinkle. Twinkle was always asking questions.

"Horses walk in a line to go to the pasture to eat," said Caleb. Caleb showed them how.

Sasha yawned. Caleb walked as slowly as he talked.

All the horses watched Caleb—except Sasha. She watched a butterfly flutter up and down. She watched a bumblebee buzz over a purple flower. She watched a red-tailed hawk soar through the sky. Her heart beat in time to the beating of their wings.

She imagined the world from above. Did the air taste sweeter? What would their valley look like from high up in the clouds?

If I could fly, thought Sasha, *I would spread my wings like the hawk and fly to faraway places. . . .*

"Sasha? Sasha?" Caleb's voice broke through her thoughts. "What is the answer, Sasha?"

"Uh, well . . ." Sasha flattened her ears to her head. Her face grew hot. She didn't know the answer. She hadn't heard the question.

Caleb sighed. "Sasha has her head in the clouds again."

"What's that mean?" asked Twinkle. "Her head is right here on her body."

"That means Sasha was daydreaming," explained Caleb. "Sasha, eyes on me. Okay?"

"Okay," said Sasha. She tried to pay attention. She really did, but her skin itched—right by the white patch on her back. That itch made her want to move, run, and soar. She looked up at the sky. She wished her head really *were* in the clouds.

CHAPTER 3) The Big Sneeze

"Everyone, find a partner," Caleb told the class.

Hooves pounded as they all scrambled to pair up. Sasha hurried to Wyatt, but Chester was already at his side.

"I'm sorry, Sasha," said Wyatt. He and Chester were partners.

Zara and Poppy stood together. Sasha's sisters were partners.

Sasha turned to Twinkle. "Partners?" Sasha asked hopefully.

Twinkle shook her head.

"No?" Sasha gulped. "Why not?"

"You don't listen. You get into trouble a lot," said Twinkle.

"No, I don't—" started Sasha. Then she stopped. She *did* get into trouble a lot. She tried to tell Twinkle why. "Sometimes, I feel like I'm standing at the starting line of a race, waiting for the whistle to blow."

Twinkle wrinkled her nose. "What race? There's no race."

"I know." Sasha searched for the right words to make Twinkle understand. "I keep getting an itchy feeling that something exciting is about to happen. It makes me fidget. I can't pay attention. Then I get into trouble."

"I need a good partner," Twinkle told her. "I want to get a good grade."

"I'll listen. I promise," said Sasha. "Please, can we be partners?"

"Okay." Twinkle smiled, and her brown eyes twinkled. That was how she'd gotten her name.

"Partners need to walk nose to tail," Caleb told the class. "Choose who is in the front and who is in the back."

"I'll be in front," said Twinkle.

"I'll be in back," agreed Sasha.

"Both partners must stay in step with each other," said Caleb. "Walk together around the pine tree, around the log, and past the big, flat rock."

"That isn't hard," Sasha told Twinkle.

They set off. Sasha kept a close watch on Twinkle's hooves. She stepped at the same time that Twinkle stepped.

"Right, left, right," said Twinkle. They walked around the pine tree.

Swish! Twinkle's tail brushed Sasha's face. The long hair tickled her nose. *Ah-ah-ah . . .*

Oh no! Sasha felt a sneeze coming—a big sneeze.

I'll mess up if I sneeze, she thought. *I can't do that to Twinkle.*

Sasha tried to hold in her sneeze. She pushed her tongue against her teeth. She closed her mouth. Her eyes bulged. Her nose twitched.

Could she do it?

CHAPTER 4) Up in the Air

Sasha did it! The sneeze went away.

"Look at the cute turtles on the log!" Twinkle called back to her.

Sasha couldn't see the turtles. All she could see was Twinkle's backside, and she didn't want to see that! Sasha raised her head high and saw the hawk again. She watched him make lazy circles over the big trees.

"*Psst*, Twinkle," whispered Sasha. "What do you think is beyond the big trees?"

"More trees?" guessed Twinkle.

"I think there are huge, crunchy pink-and-purple fruits. They taste sour and sweet at the same time. I think there are tall flowers. And the flowers have faces. Funny faces," said Sasha. She made a funny face too.

"You're silly, Sasha," said Twinkle. Sasha didn't think so.

"I want to go there someday. Do you want to come with me?" asked Sasha.

"Nope." Twinkle kept walking.

"Why not?" asked Sasha.

"I'm happy here. My family is here. I don't want to go anywhere else," said Twinkle.

Sasha didn't understand. Couldn't Twinkle feel that something amazing waited beyond their valley? Something way more amazing than learning to walk in a line!

Sasha loved her family and her home, but she knew they'd always be waiting here. She dreamed of exploring.

"The flat rock is coming up," said Twinkle.

Sasha spotted the rock. The patch on her back began to itch. She tried to ignore it. "Right, left, right," Sasha said.

The patch kept itching. It made her tail flick back and forth. It made her hooves go *tap, tap, tap*.

"Twinkle," she said suddenly, "let's jump *over* the rock!"

"No way!" cried Twinkle. "We'll get in trouble."

"Come on! It'll be so much fun," said Sasha.

"You promised to be a good partner." Twinkle turned to look at Sasha. Her eyes were not twinkling anymore. "Go *around* the rock—not over."

"Around," agreed Sasha. She shook her head to shake away the feeling, but her body still wanted to soar over the rock. One big leap. Up, up, up.

No, she scolded herself. *Friends keep promises.* Sasha wanted to be a good friend—and a good partner. She stayed behind Twinkle. Then she couldn't help it. She stepped out of line.

"Sasha!" Twinkle exclaimed, as she twisted to look at Caleb. "Get back in line!"

Sasha's legs kept moving. Her white patch itched. The itching made her legs go faster. She trotted past Twinkle. Then she cantered by Caleb.

Caleb frowned. Wyatt laughed. The other horses whispered.
  "Stop!" called Twinkle.

Sasha knew she was in big trouble, but she couldn't make herself stop. Her hooves left the ground. She leaped high over the big, flat rock. A soft wind blew through her mane. The wind grew stronger. It swirled around her. It pulled her up toward the clouds.

What's happening? Sasha wondered as she squeezed her eyes shut.

Bam! Her hooves landed back on the ground.

Sparkle!

Sasha opened her eyes. She trotted, kicking up some dirt. Then she slowed. Her heart raced from leaping.

"Sasha!" Caleb scolded. "What was that?"

Everyone in the class watched as Caleb slowly walked over to her. Sasha gulped. *Here comes trouble,* she thought.

"I'm so sorry. I didn't mean to jump," said Sasha.

"Those are your legs, right?" asked Caleb. "Your brain tells your legs what to do."

"It didn't feel that way." Sasha tried to explain. "I got this feeling . . . this itching that started on my back . . . and then I just had to jump."

Caleb widened his eyes.

"Yeah, right!" Chester laughed. He didn't believe her. No one did.

Sasha wished she were better at explaining. How could she say that she'd felt as if the clouds were calling to her? That sounded so . . . silly.

"You didn't follow my directions, Sasha," said Caleb. "You get a zero today."

Twinkle gasped. "Me too?"

"Please! It's not Twinkle's fault," Sasha told Caleb. "She should get a good grade. She's great at walking in line."

"You're right. Only you will get the bad grade," said Caleb.

Sasha turned to Twinkle to say she was sorry for being a bad partner, but Twinkle turned away. "Class is over," said Caleb.

Twinkle hurried off before Sasha could stop her. Chester and the other horses hurried off too. Only Wyatt and her sisters stayed.

"I thought you were funny, Sasha," said Wyatt.

Sasha hung her head. She hadn't wanted to be funny. She'd wanted to be a good partner. She wished she could have a do-over.

"Why couldn't you just stay in line like everyone else?" asked Zara.

"Sasha always has to be different,"
Poppy pointed out.

"It's better to be different than boring,"
said Wyatt.

"Humph!" said Poppy. She didn't
believe Wyatt.

Sasha sighed. She didn't want to be
boring, but she didn't want to get into
trouble, either.

Just then Sasha heard a squawking sound. A group of ducks flew across the sky. The ducks flew in the shape of a *V*. Sasha spotted an empty space in the *V*. She wished she could be up there too.

No! That's crazy, she told herself. *You're a horse—not a bird!*

"Sasha, look!" cried Zara. "You're sparkling!"

Sasha gasped. Silver sparkles crackled on her white patch.

"That's so cool!" cried Wyatt.

"Does it hurt?" asked Poppy.

"Not at all." Sasha couldn't stop staring. She *was* sparkling!

CHAPTER 6) The Big Secret

Her patch quickly stopped sparkling. *Why did it do that?* Sasha wondered.

She hurried to find her mom at the stream. The stream flowed down from the mountains. Cool water bubbled over the rocks. Sasha's mom took a drink.

Her dad talked nearby with Wyatt's mom. All the families in the valley lived together in a group called a herd. Wyatt's mom was the head of their herd. Sasha's dad's job was to find the best grass for the herd to eat.

"What's wrong, sweetie?" Sasha's mom gave her a gentle nuzzle. Her mom always knew when she was sad or confused.

"I'm not like the other horses here," said Sasha.

"That's a great thing. You have a spark," said her mom.

Sasha jolted. "What?" *Does she know?* she wondered.

"A spark means you have much more energy." Her mom grinned. "You're my little firecracker."

Sasha liked when her mom called her that. Her mom didn't know, after all. Sasha took a deep breath. "No one else has a white patch like mine."

"Your cloud," said her mom.

"My cloud?" asked Sasha.

"I've always thought your patch looked like a fluffy, white cloud," said her mom.

Sasha twisted her neck. Her mom was right. It really did look as if she were carrying a cloud on her back!

"Why am I the only one who has it?" asked Sasha.

"You're special," her mom said. "You should be proud."

"I know that other horses have markings, like how Dad has white socks on his legs," said Sasha. "But my patch is different. My patch was sparkling today!"

"Sparkling?" cried her mom.

Sasha's dad's ears perked up. He left Wyatt's mom and hurried over.

"It was sparkling," her mom told him quietly.

"It is time to tell her our secret," whispered her dad.

"Now?" asked her mom. "Are you sure?"

"Yes. She is old enough," whispered her dad.

"Old enough for what? What secret?" asked Sasha.

"Shh!" said her parents. They nodded toward Wyatt's mom, still nearby. They didn't want her to hear.

Sasha couldn't believe it. Her parents had a secret—and it was about her!

CHAPTER 7

The Story of Sasha

"What secret?" Sasha asked her parents again.

They had walked to a small waterfall at the far end of the stream. The rush of water blocked their voices. No one could listen now.

"You were not born in Verdant Valley like all the other horses in our herd," began her mom.

"Oh." Sasha had thought the secret would be a lot more exciting. "Where was I born?"

Sasha had heard there were different valleys. Maybe she had been born in one of them.

"We don't know," said her dad. "You were a gift."

"A gift?" Sasha giggled. "Like a present with wrapping paper and a bow?"

"Sort of," said her mom.

"That's why you're so special," said her dad.

Sasha was confused. "I don't get it."

"Follow me," said her dad. "I'll show you."

Sasha's dad led them across the valley. He stopped at the bottom of Mystic Mountain, which was the tallest mountain. Its peak reached high into the clouds.

"I'll tell you the story of baby Sasha," he said.

Sasha swallowed hard. She was excited and nervous at the same time.

"One night there was a huge storm," he began. "The sky was dark. Rain poured down. Thunder boomed."

"We huddled here to stay dry." Her mom pointed to a nook in the side of the mountain. A rock jutted out to make a roof. "We had Zara and Poppy with us. They were just babies."

"Then the biggest bolt of lightning cut through the sky. We had never seen lightning like this. It turned the sky into a rainbow of sparkling colors," said her dad.

"A minute later, we heard a cry," said her mom. "We hurried out into the rain."

"A newborn foal was wrapped in a golden blanket," said her dad. "She was beautiful. And she had a white patch on her back."

"And for a moment, the patch sparkled," added her mom.

"Was that me?" asked Sasha.

"That was you," they both said.

"But where did I come from?" Sasha looked up at the tall mountain.

"We don't know. We searched and searched in the storm. There were no other horses around," said her mom. "It was a mystery."

"There was a note on your blanket." Her dad walked to a small pile of rocks. "We saved it."

He pushed the rocks aside. A piece of paper lay underneath. It was dirty, but they could still see the words.

Sasha read the note aloud.

Please keep Sasha safe until we can see her again.

She had so many questions. They swirled in her head. "Who left me here? When are they coming back?" she asked.

Her mom and dad didn't know. They had taken Sasha in and cared for her as their own daughter. They told everyone that she was found all alone in the storm.

"We didn't tell anyone about the strange lightning or your golden blanket with the note," said her dad. "Not even Zara and Poppy."

"You are part of our family. We will always love you. We will always keep you safe." Her mom pulled Sasha close.

"The secret is yours now," said her dad. "You can tell or not tell. It's up to you."

Sasha didn't want Zara and Poppy to know how different she really was. "I'm going to keep it secret," she said.

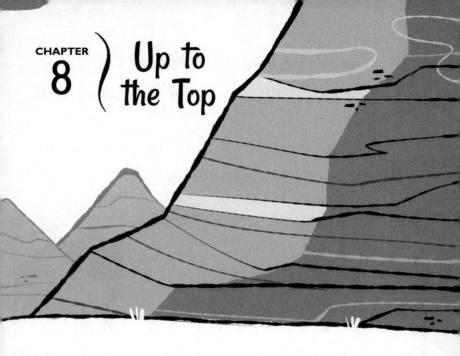

Up to the Top

"Sasha, you're not even trying!" Wyatt called out the next morning.

They were playing Catch-the-Tail. It was her favorite game. Wyatt stood right behind her. She could have easily reached out and grabbed his tail—but she didn't. She was staring up at Mystic Mountain.

Did I come from up there? she wondered.

"Let's go up the mountain," she told Wyatt.

"Why?" asked Wyatt. They had never gone up the mountain before.

"Because—" Sasha almost blurted out her secret. "Because there are wildflowers at the top to eat," she said instead.

"Let's go." Wyatt never turned down food.

They began to climb. The path was rocky.

"Did you ask your mom about the sparkling?" asked Wyatt.

"She told me—oops!" Sasha pressed her lips closed. "I can't tell you."

"Why not?" he asked.

"It's a secret," said Sasha.

"I love secrets!" cried Wyatt. "Give me a hint."

"No way." Sasha was bursting to tell him, but she was worried he wouldn't be able to keep her secret. "Let's play Follow-the-Leader. I'll be the leader." Sasha hoped a game would take Wyatt's mind off of her secret.

Sasha ate a leaf from a low-hanging branch. Wyatt ate a leaf too.

"Come on. Tell me the secret," said Wyatt.

Sasha kept her lips zipped.

She flicked her tail to greet a mountain goat. Wyatt flicked his tail too.

They climbed higher and higher. The path snaked around the mountain.

Sasha crushed red berries with her hoof. She smeared them to draw a big S.

"Your turn," she told Wyatt.
Wyatt drew a W with his crushed berries.

"Hey! The leader drew an S," Sasha pointed out.

"*W* is for Wyatt," said Wyatt, "but *S* is for secret. I'll draw an *S* if you tell me the secret."

"I can't, Wyatt," Sasha said.

Wyatt bent down to bite a purple flower. "These flowers are yummy."

"Don't eat them," said Sasha.

"Why not? You said we were looking for flowers, and I'm hungry," Wyatt said.

"We need to go to the top of the mountain," she said. "There will be better flowers there." She began to climb.

Wyatt snorted and climbed after her. "I know your secret," called Wyatt.

Oh no! she thought. "You do?" she asked.

"You're bossy." He laughed. Sasha tried to laugh too, but her white patch had started to itch. What did that mean? Was something going to happen?

"I'm the leader now." Wyatt walked in front. "Follow me!"

He hurried around a path. Sasha followed. She peeked over the edge of the mountain. Their herd looked like tiny dots in the field below. The ground was a long way down.

Wyatt jumped over a bush.

Sasha jumped, but
her jump was too
big. *"Aaahhhh!"* Sasha
tumbled through the
air. She had jumped
right off the mountain!

Wind rushed at her. Sasha's body
spun around, making her dizzy. And
then she stopped spinning. Sasha
looked down. The ground was still far
below. She passed over the stream and
then over the waterfall.

Whoa! I'm moving, she thought. *But
how?*

Sasha turned her head and gasped.
Two huge wings had sprouted from the
patch of white on her back. "I'm flying!"
cried Sasha.

CHAPTER 9) Flying!

Sasha flew through the air. The feathers in her wings sparkled in the sun. Her mane glittered.

At first she didn't know how to steer.
She flew in a crazy zigzag across the
sky. She was scared.

Then Sasha flapped her wings. She used the wind to push her forward. She began to fly smoothly. She flew fast. She flew slow. She did a fancy loop the loop. Rainbows exploded from her tail.

Sasha giggled. Flying was more fun than galloping! Flying was amazing!

She circled back to Mystic Mountain and landed at the very top. She looked around. The only one here was a goat. He was surprised to see a flying horse!

Sasha twisted to look at her wings.
They were gone!

Sasha puzzled over this. What made
her wings come, and what made them
go away?

"Sasha!" Wyatt called. He was looking
for her.

Sasha's stomach twisted. She had forgotten all about Wyatt while she was flying. Wyatt was her better-than-best friend. He never cared that she was different from the other horses—but wings and flying were *very, very* different.

Maybe he didn't see me fly, Sasha thought.

"There you are!" Wyatt hurried up to her.

"Hi!" Sasha tried to act as if nothing had happened. "What's up?"

"What's up?" cried Wyatt. "*You* were up! I saw you. You can fly!"

Sasha held her breath. She was scared. Would he make fun of her? Would he not want to be her friend? "What do you think?" she asked.

"I think it's amazing!" cried Wyatt.
"You can go anywhere!"

"You're right!" Sasha nodded at the
forest of tall trees. "I can fly beyond the
trees now."

"Will you go explore?" asked Wyatt.

"For sure." Sasha looked out at the big blue sky. She had always wanted to explore. "But, Wyatt, do you promise not to tell anyone?"

"You can trust me!" Wyatt said.

Sasha relaxed a little. "I wonder if there are other horses like me out there," she said. "Horses that can fly."

Suddenly, she knew what she would do. Sasha smiled. "I'm going to find them."

Tales of
SASHA

#2

Journey
Beyond
the Trees

by Alexa Pearl   illustrated by Paco Sordo

Contents

CHAPTER 1

Show Me Your Wings

"Guess what!" cried Sasha.

Her hooves kicked up clumps of grass as she trotted across the field. She stopped in front of her two sisters, Zara and Poppy. They stood in the shade of the big cottonwood tree.

"Guess what!" she cried again. Sasha was terrible at keeping secrets.

Zara didn't answer. She was busy. "Away . . . play . . . say . . . ," she said quietly. She was writing a poem. She needed the perfect rhyming word.

Poppy didn't answer. She was busy too. Poppy swatted flies with her tail. The flies flew around the flowers in her long mane.

Sasha let out a whinny. She hated when her sisters didn't listen to her.

Zara was the oldest sister. She had a jet-black coat and a chestnut-brown mane and tail. Poppy was the middle sister. She had a chestnut-brown coat and a jet-black mane and tail. Sasha was the youngest sister. She was all gray, except for a white patch on her back. She always felt like the plain sister, but not today.

Today, Sasha felt superspecial, and she had to tell her sisters why. Her secret was too exciting to keep to herself. "I have wings!" cried Sasha.

That did it. Zara spoke up. "You don't have wings. You're a horse, not a bird."

"I'm a horse with wings," said Sasha. Poppy laughed. "Is this a game?"

"No! This is real," said Sasha. "Yesterday, Wyatt and I hiked to the top of Mystic Mountain."

"Why did you and Wyatt go up there?" asked Zara.

"We went to eat wildflowers," said Sasha, "but I fell off the mountain!" Sasha shivered, remembering how scared she'd felt. "Wings popped out from the white patch on my back. Real wings!" cried Sasha. "I flew around and around."

Zara snorted. "You're making that up. Where are they now?"

"I'm telling the truth," said Sasha. "My wings went away after I flew back to the mountain."

"I want to see them," said Poppy. "Show us your wings."

Sasha had always known she was different from the horses in their valley. She dreamed of visiting far-off places. She ran the fastest and jumped the highest. Now she was different in the most amazing way. She had wings!

Sasha walked into the open field. She watched the birds flutter in the sky.

Come out, wings, she thought.

She waited.

"Wings, wings, wings," she repeated.

Nothing happened.

Maybe I need to move, she thought. Sasha began to trot.

No wings came out.

She looked over at her sisters. Zara listed more rhyming words. "Stay . . . way . . ." Poppy swatted a fly with her tail. They didn't believe she had wings.

She had to show them! She ran faster.

Still no wings.

Suddenly, she had the worst thought. *What if my wings never come out again?*

Sasha picked up speed. She galloped past Caleb, her teacher at school. Sasha couldn't slow down to say hello.

She raced past a group of trees. She spotted a large branch on the ground, and her white patch began to itch. She knew this feeling. Her white patch itched when her body wanted to jump. Her legs sprang off the ground. A cool breeze flowed through her mane as she soared high over the branch.

Sasha didn't come back down.

She looked to the left and saw clouds.
She looked to the right and saw birds.
She looked at her back—and saw two
beautiful wings!

"She's flying!" her sisters cried from
down below. "Sasha can really fly!"

CHAPTER 2) Watch Me Fly!

Sasha flapped her wings again and again. The silver feathers sparkled in the sunlight. She wasn't the plain sister anymore!

She flapped faster, and her body tilted sideways. The valley swirled below her, making her dizzy. Whoa! She took a deep breath and straightened. She flapped her wings more slowly, letting her body glide. She flew in a huge circle. She darted through a cloud. Sasha was having so much fun!

Sasha waved her tail at her sisters on the ground. They waved their tails back at her.

Sasha lowered her neck and came in for a bumpy landing. Her hooves kicked up a spray of dirt.

Zara and Poppy crowded around. "That was amazing!" cried Zara.

"Hey, Zara, maybe it's a sister thing," said Poppy. "Watch me fly!"

Poppy trotted. Then, with a burst of energy, she flung herself at the sky. She stretched her legs out to the side and— *splat*! She landed in a split on the ground.

Zara helped Poppy up. "I guess it's not a sister thing."

Poppy touched Sasha's wings with her nose. In a flash, Sasha's wings disappeared into her back.

"You're magic!" cried Poppy. "Make them come out again."

"It doesn't work that way," said Sasha.

"How does it work?" asked Zara.

"I have no idea," said Sasha. A lot about flying and having wings didn't make sense to her.

Zara nuzzled Sasha. "Maybe they'll come out if I press you here . . . or here . . ."

"You're tickling me!" Sasha said with a giggle. Then she became serious. Should she tell them her secret story? Zara and Poppy were her sisters, after all.

"I can fly because I don't come from here," Sasha told them.

"That's crazy. Our herd has always lived in Verdant Valley," said Zara. "Ask Mom and Dad."

"I did," said Sasha. "They told me about the day I came here. There was a big storm. You were both babies, and Mom and Dad huddled with you under Mystic Mountain to keep out of the rain. Then there was a flash of lightning, and I appeared on the ground. I was wrapped in a golden blanket, and this note was with me."

Sasha pushed aside a pile of rocks under the cottonwood tree and pulled out the note.

Zara read it aloud. "'Please keep Sasha safe until we can see her again.'"

Poppy was confused. "Who wrote that? Where did you come from?"

Sasha shrugged. She had so many questions and no answers.

"Let's find Mom and Dad," said Zara. "They're at the Drinking Place."

The three sisters hurried over to the stream. The stream started high up on Mystic Mountain and flowed down into their valley. The cool water tasted best at the Drinking Place, where the stream divided into two. Their herd gathered here, especially when the weather was warm.

Sasha spotted their mom and dad.
They were alone.

"Sasha can fly!" cried Zara and Poppy.
Her parents were excited and proud.

"Tell us how," said her dad. He knew how the flowers grew and how the bees made honey. He liked to understand how things worked.

"I don't know," said Sasha. "My wings didn't come with instructions."

"Well, someone must know," said Zara.

Her mom shook her head. "Our herd has never known a flying horse."

Sasha's ears pricked up. She heard hoof beats. "Who's there?" she called.

Caleb stepped off the path and came to her. "I saw you fly!"

Sasha gulped. Was she in trouble? "You're not the only one, Sasha," said Caleb. "Other horses can fly."

"You—you can fly?" Sasha asked Caleb.

"Not me," said Caleb. "I once met a horse who could fly."

Sasha was so happy. She wasn't the only one! "Really? When?"

"I was just a foal," said Caleb.

Sasha looked at Caleb. His copper coat was turning gray. His back sloped with old age. He had been a foal a long time ago!

Caleb told his story. "I was playing by myself near the big trees. Suddenly, a foal with wings dropped from the sky! Her wing was hurt and that made her fall. I patched her up with bark and tree sap."

Sasha's mom nodded. Caleb was known for his kindness.

"Did she have wings like mine?" asked Sasha.

"Yes. Her wings were bright blue, and her name was Sapphire," said Caleb. "She was my friend."

"What happened to Sapphire?" asked Sasha's dad.

"Her wing healed quickly. She left that night. I never saw her again." Caleb looked sad. "I told my friends and family about her. No one believed me. They thought I was making her up."

"You weren't. She was real!" cried Sasha. "Like me!"

"She was like you. You both have the same sparkly spirit. You both dream big dreams," said Caleb. "I've always liked that about you."

Sasha was surprised. Caleb often scolded her in class for daydreaming or not following the rules. She had been sure Caleb didn't like her.

"I have so many questions for Sapphire. I have to find her!" Sasha searched the sky.

"When Sapphire left, she didn't fly. She walked through the big trees," said Caleb.

Sasha hurried in the direction of the big trees.

"No! You can't go there."
Her mother blocked her path.

"Why not?" asked Sasha, but she already knew the answer. The horses in Verdant Valley had a strict rule: Never go beyond the big trees. No one could ever tell her what was back there.

"It's just the way it is," said her mother.

"Besides, you're too little to go anywhere alone," said her father.

Sasha wouldn't give up. "Someone could come with me." Other flying horses were out there somewhere. She just knew it.

"Plus, you don't know how to find her," added her mother.

"I may know," said Caleb. "Sapphire gave me a gift before she left. She asked me not to show it to anyone, but I will show Sasha now."

He began to walk slowly through the tall grass. Sasha's parents nodded for her to follow. They stayed behind with Zara and Poppy.

Sasha walked alongside Caleb. It wasn't easy to walk as slowly as he did. On the way, she told him the story of how she'd come to the valley.

Finally, he stopped at an old pine tree. The tree had a large, dark hole in its trunk. Caleb plunged his head all the way inside.

Sasha heard rustling noises. Were those leaves? Then she heard a screech. Did he wake a sleeping owl?

"Caleb! Are you okay?" cried Sasha.

He pulled his head out. Sasha's eyes grew wide.

Between his teeth, he held a brilliant blue feather. Its glittery tip crackled with silver light.

"That feather belonged to Sapphire," whispered Sasha.

4) The Magical Map

Caleb placed Sapphire's blue feather on the grass. A piece of gold fabric was wrapped around the feather's stem. A thin chain held the fabric in place, and a tiny bell hung on the chain.

Caleb unhooked the chain with his teeth. The bell rang. Suddenly, a corner of the fabric poked up. Twisting and turning, the fabric began to unroll off the feather—all by itself!

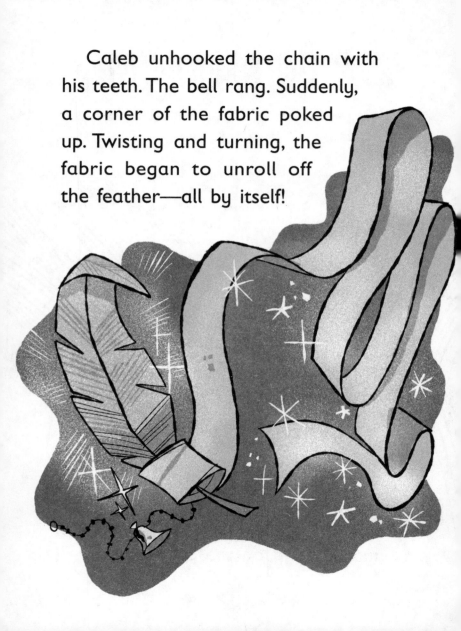

Sasha watched with her mouth open. The tiny piece of fabric grew bigger and bigger. Soon, a huge sheet of gauzy gold floated in the sunlight.

"Look!" cried Caleb.

Pictures magically lifted off the fabric. Buds blossomed into huge flowers. Strawberries, oranges, lemons, limes, and blueberries let out bursts of color that turned into a rainbow. Butterflies and fairies spun in dizzy circles. Sasha heard the rush of cool water and the sweet melody of a flute.

"What's this?" she asked.

"It's a magical map," said Caleb.

"A map of where?" Sasha had never seen this kind of color and beauty around here.

"Someplace far away," said Caleb. "Sapphire gave it to me. She said to first go through the big trees, and then follow the map to where she lives."

"Does the map work?" asked Sasha.

"I've never found out," said Caleb.

"You didn't go look for Sapphire?" Sasha was surprised.

"I tried once." Caleb snorted angrily. "I couldn't get through the big trees, because they were pushed together to make a wall. They wouldn't let me pass."

Sasha's stomach twisted. This was terrible news. "How can I find Sapphire if I can't walk through the trees?" she asked.

"You're not from our valley. You weren't born here. Maybe the trees will let you through," said Caleb.

Sasha felt hopeful. "Will you come with me?"

"The trees wouldn't let me in," Caleb reminded her.

"Maybe they'll let us go together. Please?" begged Sasha.

Caleb didn't answer right away. Instead, he lifted the tiny bell and rang it. *Whoosh!* The flute stopped playing. The floating pictures disappeared. The golden fabric shrunk and wrapped itself back around the stem of the blue feather.

Caleb hooked the chain to keep the magical map in place. He tucked the feather behind Sasha's left ear.

"We're going to need this map later," he said.

"We?" asked Sasha. Her heart beat quickly.

"Yes." Caleb shook his head, as if he couldn't believe he was doing this. "I'll meet you tomorrow at sunrise."

"We're going to find Sapphire!" Sasha did a little dance. "Thank you!"

"Don't thank me yet," warned Caleb. "First, we'll need to make it through the trees."

Sasha nuzzled her mom early the next morning as the first rays of sun broke through the darkness. Her sisters slept nearby. Her dad was already out looking for grazing pastures for the herd.

"Come home soon," whispered her mother. She slicked back Sasha's forelock with her tongue. "I'll be waiting for you. We all will. We love you."

"I love you too." Sasha nuzzled closer. For a moment, she thought about staying under the cottonwood tree with her family. Then she felt Sapphire's feather tucked behind her ear. This was her big chance to find other flying horses. *I have to be brave*, she thought.

Sasha set off across the field. The grass was damp with morning dew. No horses were grazing this early.

Sasha spotted Caleb up ahead. Then she stopped. Who was standing next to Caleb? She trotted closer.

"Wyatt!" she cried. "What are *you* doing here?"

"Poppy told me what you're up to. My dad said I could go too," said Wyatt. "Best friends always have adventures together."

"That's true!" Sasha was glad Wyatt was coming with them.

"Are you ready?" Caleb asked them.

"Yeah!" cried Wyatt.

Sasha nodded. She didn't want to tell them that she felt a little scared.

Caleb walked forward. Wyatt walked behind him. Sasha walked behind Wyatt. Leaves and twigs crunched under their hooves. Sunlight peeked through the branches overhead. Birds sang in the treetops. Sasha hummed along. They walked for a long time.

Suddenly, it became quiet. The birds had stopped singing. The sky turned dark.

Sasha looked up and gasped. The branches stretched toward one another, blocking the sun. "G-g-guys, the trees are moving!" cried Sasha.

The tree trunks lined up side by side. They made a wall.

Caleb tried to walk forward, but he was pushed back. He tried again and again. "I can't do it." Sweat dripped into his eyes. "You need to try, Sasha."

Sasha shivered. She took a tiny step forward.

"Keep going!" called Wyatt.

Sasha took another step. Then another and another. The sun began to shine again. The birds began to sing again.

She was doing it! The trees were parting. They were letting her through!

"I see the way. Grab on to my tail," she called to Wyatt and Caleb. "I can lead us."

"I can't go," said Caleb.

Sasha whirled around. "What's wrong?"

"My knees hurt. I'm tired," he said. "I will only slow you down."

"No way! I need you," cried Sasha.

Caleb shook his head. "Not anymore. The trees opened for you. You have Wyatt. You have the map. I'll rest here. You will be fine."

Sasha's heart pounded. She'd never gone anywhere on her own. She didn't even understand how the map worked.

Wyatt nudged her forward. "I'd bet Sapphire is right on the other side of the trees."

Sasha felt her white patch itch. It only did that when her body wanted to go. Did that mean the flying horses really were near?

she made up her mind. "We can do this," she told Wyatt. Wyatt held on to her tail with his teeth. Together, they walked toward the trees.

Help Is on the Way

The trees moved to let them pass.

"We're doing it!" Sasha called to Wyatt.

Wyatt didn't answer. He didn't dare let go of her tail.

Sasha walked faster. She wanted to get them out of the creepy woods quickly. Finally, they stepped into a field of wildflowers.

"It's beautiful!" cried Sasha. The flowers pulsed with neon colors that were almost too bright for her eyes.

"It's delicious!" cried Wyatt. He began to munch. Wyatt loved to eat flowers.

Sasha danced in and out of the electric flowers. She bent down to smell them.

"Wyatt!" she cried. "The red flowers smell like cherry. The yellow flowers smell like lemon. The pink flowers smell like cotton candy."

"They taste like how they smell," called Wyatt. His mouth was full of flowers.

"We need to find Sapphire," Sasha said to remind Wyatt. She pulled the blue feather from behind her ear. She opened the chain, and the tiny bell rang. The golden map magically unwrapped in the air.

"What do you see?" called Wyatt.

Sasha puzzled over the picture shimmering in front of her. "It's blue and moving. I see waves. It must be water."

"It's a lake." Wyatt came over. "There's an arrow on the lake. That arrow means we need to go across the lake."

Sasha turned in a circle. "What lake?"

"Over there." Wyatt pointed to a lake at the end of the flower field. "Race you. On your mark, get set—"

"Go!" Sasha took off.

Wyatt was fast, but she was faster. They galloped to the shore of a big lake.

Wyatt dipped his hoof into the warm water. "This lake is huge. We can't swim across."

"I could try to fly across," said Sasha.

"What about me?" asked Wyatt. "Could I hold on to your tail and fly too?"

"I don't think so." Trying to fly with Wyatt sounded hard. She'd surely crash.

"I won't leave you behind," she promised. Then she sighed. "We're stuck."

"We need help," agreed Wyatt.

"Help is on the way!"

"Who said that?" asked Wyatt.

Sasha pointed. Something was moving across the lake toward them.

Wyatt squinted. "It looks like a huge raft."

"It's a raft made out of tree trunks," said Sasha.

They watched the raft move closer and closer. Three beavers stood on the raft. They paddled it up to the shore.

"Ahoy!" called a beaver wearing a navy captain's hat. "Are you here for the noon crossing?"

"Is it noon?" asked Sasha. She had never been good at telling time.

"The sun is high. It's time to sail," said the captain. "Be quick. Hop on."

Sasha turned to Wyatt. "Should we?"

"Let's do it!" Wyatt stepped onto the raft.

"Why not?" Sasha joined him.

"Onward!" called the captain. All three beavers began to paddle, and the raft glided across the lake.

"Did Sapphire send you?" Sasha asked the captain hopefully.

"No one sent me," he said. "The ferry is on a schedule. It goes every hour. Sometimes every two hours. Sometimes I take a nap. Then it doesn't go."

"That doesn't sound like a good schedule," said Sasha.

"I'm glad it wasn't nap time," Wyatt pointed out. "Sasha wanted to fly, but I can't."

The captain poked Sasha with his paddle. "You're a winged one!"

"You've seen them!" cried Sasha. That was a good sign. "Where are they?"

"I'm a water-and-wood guy. I don't know what happens in the sky." He began to paddle again.

"Row, row, row, your boat," he sang. The other beavers joined in. Their oars pushed through the water as they sang.

When the song ended, the captain steered the raft to a dock. He hurried Sasha and Wyatt off. A family of foxes got on.

"Wait!" called Sasha. The captain hadn't told her where to go.

"Ticktock!" called the captain. "No time to chat." The three beavers paddled the raft away.

"I hope the flying horses are close by," Sasha told Wyatt. "Let's check the map."

She unhooked the chain. The bell rang, and the magic map opened. Sasha reared back. Hundreds of eyes swirled before them! Blinking. Winking. Staring. Eyes were everywhere.

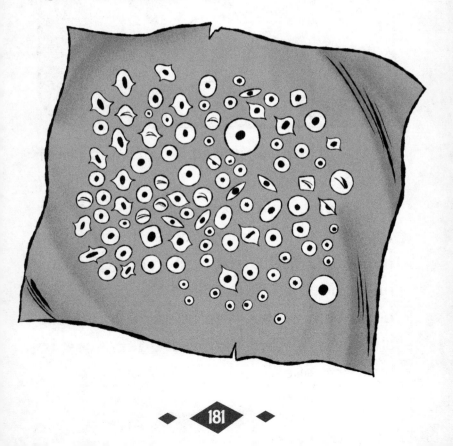

Wyatt squeezed his eyes shut. "I don't like all those eyes looking at me. Maybe we should try to go back."

Sasha was surprised. Wyatt had never acted scared before.

"I can't give up now," she said. The thought of the flying horses nearby had made her feel braver. She rang the tiny bell and the map rolled up again. The eyes went away. "We need to find eyes," she told Wyatt. "I need your eyes to look for eyes."

Wyatt opened one eye and then the other. Then he followed Sasha. She walked in front.

They passed three rabbits playing hopscotch.

They passed two flamingos on a tightrope.

They passed a turtle flying a kite.

"I knew beyond the trees would be special," said Sasha.

"This place is nothing like home," said Wyatt.

Suddenly, she stopped short. Wyatt tumbled into her.

"All eyes on me!" cried a bright blue peacock. He strutted before them. "Do you see what I see?"

"What does he see?" Sasha whispered to Wyatt.

"You need more eyes to see what I see," said the large bird.

"More eyes?" Wyatt didn't like the sound of that.

The peacock lifted his tail and opened a huge fan of emerald-green feathers. Each feather had an eye-shaped spot in the middle.

"He has eyes on his feathers!" cried Wyatt. "The map wanted us to find this peacock."

"Do you know where Sapphire is?" asked Sasha.

"Look and see." The peacock grinned. "A bird's-eye view is always best."

"Everything is a riddle here," Wyatt said with a grumble.

Sasha looked closely. Every feather looked the same—except one. One feather was bright blue, not green. It didn't have an eye-shaped spot. It looked exactly like the feather Sapphire had given Caleb.

"That feather isn't yours," she told the peacock. "That feather comes from the wing of a flying horse!"

Behind the Gold Door

Sasha plucked the blue feather from the peacock's tail. It had a square stem.

"Follow the feather to the winged horses," said the peacock. Then he strutted away.

"There isn't a map on this feather," said Wyatt. "How do we follow it?"

Suddenly, a strong breeze blew the feather from Sasha's mouth. The feather twirled in crazy circles. Then it zoomed forward.

For a moment, Sasha watched it. Then she remembered the peacock's words. "Follow the feather!" cried Sasha. She raced after it.

"Wait for me!" yelled Wyatt.

The feather flew to a beach. They galloped down the hot sand after it. Finally, the feather fluttered to the ground. Sasha and Wyatt stopped too. They stood in a clearing surrounded by rock walls. The sand glittered with rubies, emeralds, diamonds, and other jewels.

"Wow! My sisters would love it here," said Sasha.

Wyatt pointed to a shiny gold door
in one of the rock walls. "What's that?"

Sasha walked over to it and knocked.

No answer.
She knocked harder.

Still no answer.

She pushed against it. "It's locked," she told Wyatt.

Wyatt looked at the sky. "The sun is going down. We should go home."

"Go home? Now?" Sasha couldn't believe it. "We've made it through the big trees, crossed a huge lake, and now we're here. Maybe Sapphire and the flying horses are on the other side of this door. I can't go home now!"

She unhooked the magic map and watched it unroll. A picture of an old-fashioned key floated before them. "We need to find a key," said Sasha. "A key will open the door."

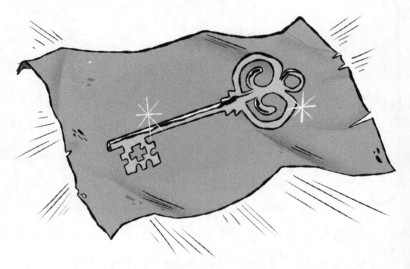

Wyatt paced back and forth. "It'll be dark soon. Do you think the ferry is still running? Do you think Caleb is still by the trees?"

"Let's look fast," said Sasha. "Hurry!"

Sasha and Wyatt searched for a key in the piles of rubies and emeralds. They couldn't find one anywhere.

"We need to go," said Wyatt.

"Soon." Sasha wouldn't stop digging.

Wyatt groaned and kicked at a pile. A diamond sailed through the air and hit the gold door.

Sasha hurried over to the door. "Oh! You scratched it." Then she spotted a tiny hole. She knew that shape! "I found the keyhole. Where's the blue feather from the peacock?" she asked.

Wyatt lifted it from the ground and brought it over. "Why do you want this? Don't we need a key?"

"The feather is the key," she said.

She stuck the tip of the feather's square stem into the keyhole. *Click!*

The gold door swung
open—and a horse flew out.
Then another and another!

"We found the flying horses!" cried
Wyatt.

Sasha sucked in her breath as they
circled overhead. "They're just like me."

Wyatt looked to the sky. "That horse has yellow wings. That horse has purple wings. That horse has blue wings. It's Sapphire!"

Sasha felt her patch itch. Then every part of her body itched to fly.

"Sasha," said Wyatt, "your wings popped out!"

"Should I go up?" she asked.

"Yes! Go fly!" said Wyatt.

Sasha grinned at her best friend. Then she ran and leaped. Her wings flapped, and she soared up, up, up.

She was finally going to meet other flying horses!

#3

Tales of SASHA

A New Friend

by Alexa Pearl

illustrated by Paco Sordo

Contents

Just Like Me

"Wait for me!" cried Sasha. She tried to catch up. She flew higher. She flapped her wings faster, but she still couldn't reach them.

Thick clouds rolled in, making it hard to see. Now she didn't know which way to turn. Then Sasha's breath caught in her throat.

Three horses flew out of a large cloud! One was yellow, one was blue, and one was purple. Their colorful wings shone bright against the gray sky. They were just like her. They were horses that could fly!

Sasha had never met another flying horse before. She just *had* to talk to them—now!

The three horses darted in and out of the clouds. They flew in crazy patterns.

"Wait for me!" she called again.

The three flying horses didn't wait.

Sasha was the fastest horse in her valley. She had won every running race. But flying was different than running. Horses didn't fly in a straight line.

"Keep going!" Wyatt called to her from the beach. The sand at his hooves sparkled with magical jewels. He raised his tail in a salute.

Sasha saluted back. Wyatt was her best friend. He had traveled all the way from their home in Verdant Valley to Crystal Cove with her.

"That must be Sapphire!" Wyatt pointed at the blue horse.

Sasha flapped her wings as fast as she could. She had heard stories about Sapphire, but she'd never met her. Sasha had never met *any* flying horses. Until now, she'd thought she was the only one. She had so many questions for them.

"Sapphire! I'm back!" cried Sasha.

Sapphire swooped low and out of sight.

She didn't hear me, thought Sasha.

Then Sasha spotted the yellow horse. She sped over to him.

"I just learned to fly!" she called.

The yellow horse soared higher and out of sight.

He doesn't care, thought Sasha.

The purple horse zoomed by.

"Hello!" called Sasha.

The purple horse didn't answer. Instead, she tucked her head and somersaulted in the air.

Sasha gasped. That was amazing!

"Your turn," called the purple horse.

Sasha looked around. Who was she talking to?

The purple horse pointed her braided tail at Sasha.

"Me?" Sasha gulped. She didn't know if she could do gymnastics and fly at the same time.

The purple horse waited.

Was this a test? If she passed, would the purple horse answer her questions? Sasha took a deep breath. *You can do this,* she told herself. *Head first, legs in, tuck, and roll. Go!*

The world spun upside down. Wind rushed up her nostrils, and her stomach twisted. Then she was upright again and flying. She heard Wyatt cheer. She had done it!

The purple horse smiled. "Fly with me!" she called.

Together, they soared through the clouds. The warm wind blew their manes. Sasha smiled. She had made her first friend in the Land of Flying Horses.

A New Friend

The purple horse and Sasha glided down to the beach. Sasha's hooves kicked up a huge spray of sand and jewels as she skidded to a stop.

The purple horse laughed. "What's with your landing?"

"Sorry." Sasha bit her lip. "I just started flying."

The purple horse's violet eyes grew wide. "You *just* got your wings? So cool! I got mine last year."

Sasha admired the purple horse's shimmering wings. "Yours are so much fluffier than mine. Why?"

"I put honey on them to make them fluffy," said the purple horse.

"Really?" Sasha wrinkled her nose. That sounded gross.

"*Not* really." The purple horse laughed again. "Honey would make my feathers stick together. I made that up. There's no big secret. Your wings will grow fluffier the more you use them."

"Does that make flying easier?" asked Sasha.

"So much easier! Fluffy wings are powerful." She fanned out her wings and struck a pose. "Don't I look superpowerful?"

The purple horse laughed again. Sasha found herself laughing, too.

"I'm Kimani." The purple horse stood nose-to-nose with Sasha. "I've never seen you here in Crystal Cove."

"I'm not from here," said Sasha. "I live in Verdant Valley."

"Where's that?" asked Kimani.

"It's down the beach, over the lake, through the fields, and on the other side of the big trees," said Sasha.

"You live on the *other side* of the big trees? For real?" cried Kimani.

Sasha nodded. "I was left there when I was a baby. There was a note on my golden blanket. I don't know who left me or why. I came here to find out. My name is Sasha."

Kimani reared up on her hind legs. "*You're* Sasha?"

"You've heard of me?" Sasha's heart thumped with excitement.

Kimani looked a little nervous. "You're the *real* Sasha?"

"I guess." Sasha wasn't sure what that meant.

Kimani scanned
the sky as if she
were looking for
someone. Then she
twirled her tail.
Three twirls one
way, and then three
twirls the other way.

Sasha had never seen a tail move like that. "Is everything okay?" she asked.

Kimani quickly stopped spinning her tail. "Of course! I just, um, think the sky looks really pretty today," she replied nervously.

"Okay . . . ," Sasha said, but she wasn't convinced.

"Hey!" Kimani exclaimed. "Who's that?"

The Toucan Brings a Message

"Ouch! These red gems get hot in the sun!" Wyatt galloped toward them.

"That's my friend, Wyatt," Sasha told Kimani.

Kimani stared at him. "Didn't you get your wings yet?"

"I'm never getting wings. Horses don't have wings," said Wyatt.

"Are you sure?" Kimani spread her wings wide.

"Horses don't have wings where we come from," explained Sasha. "I was the only one."

"That sounds like a terrible place," said Kimani.

"Not at all," said Sasha. "Verdant Valley is great. We have a school and big fields to run in."

"We have a stream with cold water and a tall mountain with wildflowers," added Wyatt.

"My family is there." Sasha told Kimani about her mother, her father, and her older sisters Zara and Poppy.

"None of them have wings," Kimani pointed out. "You should stay here. Crystal Cove is the Land of Flying Horses."

"Stay here?" Now Wyatt reared back.

"Don't worry," Sasha told Wyatt. They'd left home at sunrise, and now it was sunset. Sasha missed her family. "I'm not staying. I only came to find other winged horses."

"It's getting dark." Wyatt tugged Sasha. They had a long journey back home.

"Don't leave!" Kimani looked at the sky again. "You have to wait."

At that moment, a toucan
swooped down and landed
on Kimani's back. "I got your
signal," said the
toucan.

So that's what the tail twirling was about,
thought Sasha.

"I have a message from Sapphire. She
wants to see the new horse now." The
toucan spoke in a booming voice.

Sasha turned to Wyatt. Many years ago, Sapphire had met their old teacher, Caleb. They were both foals, and Caleb had helped her when she'd hurt her wing. Before she flew away, she'd given him a magical map. Sasha and Wyatt had used that map today to find the flying horses. Wyatt knew how important meeting Sapphire was to Sasha.

Wyatt nodded. "Okay. Let's go."

"Not you," said the toucan. "Just Sasha."

"Wyatt is not one of us," explained Kimani. "He doesn't have wings."

Sasha's ears flattened against her head. The horses at home used to say she was different because she daydreamed about faraway places. Sometimes they wouldn't be her partner at school.

"I won't go without him." Sasha's voice sounded strong, but her knees felt wobbly.

Kimani shared a secret look with the toucan. Sasha was worried. Had she ruined her big chance to talk to Sapphire?

Kimani shrugged. "Okay. Wyatt can come along."

Sasha and Wyatt grinned.

The toucan led the way. The three horses headed down the beach and entered a jungle. Thick tropical plants crowded close together. Fuzzy caterpillars chewed fan-shaped leaves. Blue dragonflies swarmed above their heads. The air grew warm and sticky.

Sasha blew her forelock out of her eyes. She wished for the cool shade of the cottonwood tree back home.

Wyatt tried to munch a big flower.

"I wouldn't eat that," warned Kimani.

"Whoa!" Wyatt jumped back as a red horse poked her nose out from behind the flower.

Sasha was about to tease Wyatt for being a scaredy-cat. Then she saw them. All of them.

CHAPTER 4

Who Are You, Really?

Sasha turned slowly in a circle.

Pink. Lavender. Turquoise. Horses of all colors hid in the leafy plants. They stared at Sasha and whispered. Were they talking about her?

"What's going on?" whispered Sasha.

"They're friendly." Kimani pushed her forward. "They came to greet you."

"Me?" asked Sasha. "They don't know me."

"Everyone knows you," said Kimani.

Sasha chewed her lip. How could they know her?

"Why are they hiding?" asked Wyatt.

"They're shy, and—" Kimani didn't get to finish. A beautiful blue horse stepped into a clearing.

"Sapphire!" Sasha began to trot toward her.

"Whoa!" A yellow horse jumped out and blocked her path. "I need to check you first."

"Check me for what?" asked Sasha.

"I need to be sure you are who you say you are," he said.

"Who else would I be?" Sasha was confused.

"We should go," whispered Wyatt.

Sasha knew if she was going to get any answers, they would come from Sapphire. She locked eyes with the yellow horse. He was larger than any horse Sasha had ever met. "Fine. Check me."

He walked around Sasha. "She has a white patch on her back. It is the shape of a cloud."

A horse in the plants let out a gasp.

"I've always had that patch," said Sasha. "That's where my wings come out from."

The yellow horse looked inside her mouth. "She is missing a back tooth on the left side," he said.

"It's been missing since I was born," said Sasha.

Another horse gasped.

The yellow horse nodded at the ground behind her. "Are these your hoof prints?"

"Yes." Sasha saw for the first time that her hoof print was different from Wyatt and Kimani's. Hers had a heart shape in the middle.

"The patch, the tooth, and the hoof print all prove it," said the yellow horse. "She really is Sasha. Sasha has returned!"

The colorful herd of horses burst out of their hiding spots. With a *whoosh*, they opened their wings and let out a huge cheer. They were cheering for her!

Let's Dance

Sapphire walked toward her. "How did you find your way back to us?"

Sasha showed her the blue feather and the magical map. "You left these with Caleb."

"He saved my life." Sapphire closed her eyes, remembering him. "If he hadn't fixed my wing, I would've been in danger."

"Danger? Why?" asked Sasha.

Sapphire let out a long breath. "That's a story for another time."

Now that Sapphire was here, Sasha was nervous. Sasha decided to ask her most important question first. "The note on my blanket said: 'Please keep Sasha safe until we can see her again.' Did you write that note? Did you leave me in Verdant Valley?"

"It wasn't me," said Sapphire.

Sasha's stomach dropped. She'd been so sure it had been Sapphire.

"I did pick Verdant Valley. Caleb showed me that the horses there were kind," said Sapphire.

Sasha thought about this. "If you chose the place, does that mean you know where I came from?"

Before Sapphire could answer, music filled the air. A pink horse began to sing. Others tapped their hooves in time with the beat.

"Enjoy the party!" cried Sapphire. "It's for you. We'll talk tomorrow." She hurried away.

Fireflies filled the night sky. They spelled SASHA with their lights. A huge apple-and-carrot cake was wheeled in front of her.

"Don't you think it's strange that you're such a big deal here?" asked Wyatt.

"Maybe, but I like it." Sasha had never had a big party before. She tapped her hooves happily to the music.

"Let's dance!" Kimani lifted her body several inches off the ground.

"How do I do that?" Sasha wanted to hover like a hummingbird, too.

"It's easy." Kimani showed Sasha how to move her wings in small circles. Sasha rose off the ground.

"Time to twirl!" called Kimani. Together, they twirled above Wyatt.

"You should dance, too," called Sasha.

"I'm stuck down here," said Wyatt.

"You can dance there." Sasha wished Wyatt wasn't being such a party pooper.

Kimani and Sasha twirled until they were both dizzy.

Thwack! Wyatt's tail playfully swatted Sasha. She dropped to the ground.

"You can't do that." Kimani narrowed her eyes at Wyatt.

"I do it all the time." Wyatt was forever swatting his tail at Sasha.

"You don't get it," said Kimani. "She's *Sasha*."

"I know who she is." Wyatt turned to Sasha. "It's time to go home."

"We're having peppermint ice cream soon," said Kimani.

"That sounds yummy." Then Sasha saw Wyatt scowl. "But we need to go back."

"It's too late to leave. The ferry doesn't run after dark. Wyatt can't get across the lake," said Kimani. The lake was too wide to swim across, and Wyatt couldn't fly.

"Stay here tonight. We'll have a sleepover!" Kimani's violet eyes twinkled with excitement.

"Great idea," said Sasha.

Wyatt frowned. He didn't think so. "What about Caleb? He's waiting for us."

"No problem." Kimani waved over a firefly. She whispered in his ear, and then he flew away. "He'll bring Caleb a message right away."

Sasha and Kimani danced and danced. Wyatt stood silently near a group of other horses not dancing.

When Sasha finally took a break, Wyatt pulled her aside. "I need to talk to you."

"The ice cream is melting," called Kimani.

"Wait until later," Sasha told Wyatt. She hurried to get ice cream.

Afterward, Kimani took them to her room. All the horses lived in caves carved into the cliffs. Soft patterned blankets covered the floors and the walls. Fluffy fur pillows were scattered everywhere. Sasha loved how cozy it was.

"We can sleep over here." Wyatt pushed together two pillows.

Sasha yawned. She was tired from their long day.

"Don't sleep yet," said Kimani. "Have you ever flown in the moonlight?"

Sasha's white patch itched with excitement. It did that when her body wanted to fly. "Could I touch a star?" she asked Kimani.

"Let's try." Kimani grinned.

"What about me?" Wyatt frowned. "I wanted to talk to you, Sasha."

Sasha hated not including Wyatt, but Kimani was her first flying horse friend. Tomorrow, she would go home. No one there would fly with her through the stars. She'd have plenty of time to talk to Wyatt later.

"I'll be right back," Sasha promised him.

The world below was dark and silent as the two horses flew through the night sky. Sasha tried to touch a star. She couldn't reach it. Stars were much farther away than they looked!

Sasha waved to a snowy-white owl that glided by. She wondered if Wyatt were looking up. Did he see her tail sparking with magic in the darkness?

Together, Sasha and Kimani somersaulted in the moonlight.

Wyatt was fast asleep when they got back. Sasha didn't wake him. She went to sleep, too.

At dawn, Wyatt woke up.

"Sasha," whispered Wyatt. His breath was warm against her ear. "Sasha."

She didn't answer. She was still sleeping.

Wyatt nudged her. "It's time to go home."

Sasha opened one eye. Pale morning sunlight poked through the cave door. How could that be? She felt as if she'd just gone to bed. "Not yet," she mumbled.

Wyatt kept on nudging her.

"Go away," she grumbled. She was so tired. She closed her eyes again.

Hours later, Sasha finally woke up. Bright sunshine filled the cave.

"Hey, there." Kimani stood by the open door. "There's leftover cake. Want some?"

"Sure." Sasha stretched her legs. "Where's Wyatt?"

"He went home," said Kimani.

"He went without me?" Sasha couldn't believe it.

Kimani shrugged. "He was up early. He tried to wake you."

Sasha winced. She remembered now.

"I told him not to bother you. Besides, we don't need him. He's better off in Verdant Valley," said Kimani.

"You *told* him to go?" Sasha's voice rose.

"He wanted to go," said Kimani. "He was upset."

Sasha felt horrible. She had been so caught up with her new friend that she hadn't realized he was upset.

"I've got good news!" cried Kimani. "Sapphire has been waiting for you to wake up."

"I need to find Wyatt," said Sasha.

"He'll be fine." Kimani pointed over at the golden door where Sapphire lived. "Don't you want answers to your questions? This is your chance."

Sasha let Kimani push her toward Sapphire's home.

"Greetings!" The toucan opened the door. "Sapphire's almost ready. Please enjoy this breakfast."

He placed an enormous platter in front of Sasha. Sunflowers, marigolds, and daisies were piled high. There was one bowl filled with honey and one bowl filled with raspberry jam.

Sasha licked her lips. She leaned forward to dip a daisy into the honey.

The sweet smell made her think of Wyatt. Wyatt loved wildflowers. She remembered the day they climbed Mystic Mountain to search for the tastiest flowers and her wings had popped out for the very first time. Wyatt had been so happy for her. He had wanted her to find the flying horses. He had gone with her through the scary forest when Caleb couldn't make it. He'd been by her side the whole time. Now he was by himself. What if he didn't know how to get home? He didn't have the magic map.

Sasha spit out the flower. She couldn't stay here any longer.

"Kimani," said Sasha, "tell Sapphire I have to go."

"You can't!" cried Kimani.

"I need to make sure Wyatt is okay." Wyatt was her oldest friend. She'd been wrong to ignore him. She wasn't going to leave him alone now.

"Go with her," the toucan told Kimani.

"You don't have to." Sasha knew Kimani didn't like Wyatt all that much.

"I want to help," said Kimani. "I know this land better than you."

CHAPTER 7

Bend, Cross, Spring!

Sasha and Kimani trotted down the beach.

"Hello!" A peacock stepped out and opened his tail feathers.

"We're looking for my friend." Sasha had met this peacock yesterday.

"Eyes in the sky see so much more," said the peacock.

"We can't fly," explained Kimani. "We're searching for hoof prints. Her friend doesn't fly."

"He's heading to the big trees," said Sasha.

The peacock's feathers quivered. "You're going into the big trees, too?"

Kimani nodded.

The peacock lowered his voice. "Keep eyes open for the little ones."

Sasha wanted to ask who the little ones were, but a troop of spider monkeys rode by on scooters. Kimani stopped one to ask about Wyatt.

"He was meeting the morning ferry," said the spider monkey.

Sasha and Kimani set off at a gallop. They reached the edge of the big lake.

"Is that him on the ferry?" asked
Kimani.

Sasha squinted at the far side of the
lake. Wyatt stood on a raft that was
paddled by three beavers. They watched
him step onto the far dock and trot
away.

Sasha pawed the ground. What should she do? It would take a long time for the beavers to paddle back to pick them up.

"Let's fly," said Kimani.

Sasha stared at the water in front of her. "I can't. I need a running start to take off."

"No, you don't. Bend your knees low." Kimani showed her how. "Then cross your eyes."

"What?" That sounded so silly.

"Do you want to catch up to Wyatt?" asked Kimani.

Sasha nodded. The longer she waited, the farther away he was getting.

"Bend your knees, cross your eyes, then spring up fast," said Kimani.

Sasha bent, crossed, and sprang. She was flying! She couldn't believe how many new things Kimani had taught her in the past day.

She and Kimani flew over the lake
in minutes. Wyatt had already trotted
through the field of neon flowers. Now
he stepped into the woods
beyond the big trees.

Sasha landed and ran with a burst of speed towards Wyatt.

"Stop!" Kimani cut in front of her.

Sasha pulled back so she wouldn't crash into Kimani. "What's wrong?"

"You can't go into the woods," said Kimani. "There is danger there for flying horses."

Sasha remembered that Kimani had made up that story about honey turning wings fluffier. "You're making this up because you don't want Wyatt around."

"I'm not making it up," said Kimani. "You're my friend, and I want you to be safe. You have wings now, and others know it. There's danger for us."

What should I do? Sasha wondered. *Should I trust Kimani? Or should I follow Wyatt?*

CHAPTER

8) A Big Sneeze

Sasha dodged around Kimani. She sped toward the trees. She was fine yesterday in the woods. She was going after Wyatt.

Sasha tried to remember the path home through the woods. The trees were close together and tangled with one another.

She looked behind her. No Kimani. She was by herself. She followed the map until she spotted green fields beyond the trees—and Wyatt! He was leaving the woods.

"Wy—" She started to call for him. Then she felt pricks along her back. What was that? It felt like tiny feet were running on her back. How could that be? What was on her? She twisted to see.

Oh! Five tiny creatures stood on her back. Everything about them was pointy. Pointy nose. Pointy chin. Pointy ears. Pointy elbows and fingers. They had bright green skin and wore outfits made from leaves.

She tried to shake them off. They stayed on.

"Help!" She felt something tug at one of her wings.

Wyatt hurried back into the woods at the sound of her cries. He swatted them with his tail, but their tiny feet seemed glued to her back. Two more dropped onto her from the tree above.

"What should we do?" Sasha was scared.

"I don't know." Wyatt looked scared, too.

"Sneeze," called someone from deep in the woods.

Sasha spotted Kimani hiding behind a nearby tree.

"Come out and help," called Wyatt.

"I can't," said Kimani. "They'll get me, too. Wyatt, you need to sneeze on them."

Wyatt didn't move.

"Do it fast!" called Kimani.

This is the danger Kimani warned about, Sasha realized. *She had been telling the truth.*

"Trust her," Sasha told Wyatt.

Wyatt tried to sneeze. Only a cough came out. He tried again. The little creatures started tugging on Sasha's wings.

"I can't sneeze on command," he said.

Kimani raced from the safety of her hiding spot. She picked a dandelion from the ground. She waved it under Wyatt's nose.

A-a-choo! Wyatt let out an enormous sneeze near Sasha's back. Snot covered the little creatures and unglued their feet. They fell to the ground.

For a moment, Sasha stared at them. They were so tiny! Then they grabbed onto her tail. They began to climb it, using the hair as a rope.

Sasha's surprise turned to anger. Hot white sparks shot out of her tail, shocking the creatures. They scurried into the bushes and wrapped themselves in leaves until they couldn't be seen.

"We need to get out of here," said Kimani.

They all quickly hurried into Verdant Valley.

Two Friends

Sasha was so happy to see the green fields of home again.

"I didn't listen and left you out. I'm sorry," Sasha told Wyatt. "Is that why you left?"

Wyatt kicked at the grass. "You didn't need me. You found a new friend. I thought you wanted to stay with her."

"I'm your friend, too," said Sasha. "I *do* need you, don't you see? You just saved me."

"It wasn't only me. Kimani helped, too." Wyatt gave Kimani a shy smile. "We worked together."

Kimani smiled back. "That was a good sneeze. You've got a lot of sticky snot."

"No wings, but plenty of snot. That's me." Wyatt laughed.

"We all have something that makes us special," teased Sasha. She was lucky she'd had two good friends to help her.

"So what were those things?" Wyatt
asked Kimani.

"They're plant pixies, the enemy of flying horses. They want to steal our power of flight," said Kimani.

"How?" asked Wyatt.

"They need to pluck two wing feathers—one from the right wing and one from the left wing. The feathers fit into a harness that they wear. With both feathers in the harness, the plant pixie can fly," explained Kimani.

"I have plenty of feathers," said Sasha. "I could share some."

Kimani shook her head. "It doesn't work that way. Every time a feather is taken from a flying horse, she grows weaker. Soon, she can't fly or even gallop."

Sasha didn't like the sound of that.

"Plant pixies live in the woods," said Kimani. "A spell was placed on Verdant Valley so they can't come here. It was very important that you grew up safe."

Sasha titled her head. "I don't understand. Why did I need to be kept safe?"

"That's what I've been trying to tell you," said Wyatt. "I heard the yellow horse talking about you at the party."

"You know?" asked Kimani.

"I do," said Wyatt. "Should I tell her?"

"Tell me what?" Sasha stared at her two friends.

Wyatt and Kimani spoke at the same time. "You are the Lost Princess."

Read on for a sneak peek
from the fourth book in the
Tales of Sasha series!

Tales of
SASHA

Princess
Lessons

by Alexa Pearl
illustrated by Paco Sordo

CHAPTER 1) Little Fairy Creatures

"Did you hear that?" Sasha lifted her ears.

"Hear what?" asked her better-than-best friend, Wyatt.

"A crunch from under this boysenberry bush." Sasha stepped forward to look. "Is it them?"

"Stay back!" cried Wyatt. "I'll look."

Sasha frowned. She should look first—not Wyatt. She was the brave one. Everyone knew that.

But everything had changed this week.

She wasn't a regular horse like Wyatt anymore. She was a flying horse—and flying horses were in danger.

"Sasha! You're home!" Poppy squealed and trotted toward her sister.

There were three sisters in Sasha's family. Sasha was the youngest, Zara was the oldest, and Poppy was in the middle. Poppy was the fancy sister. She wore flowers in her mane and tail.

Sasha nuzzled Poppy. She was happy to be home in Verdant Valley. So much had happened this week. First, Sasha had discovered that she had wings and could fly. Then, she'd gone away to search for other flying horses.

"What's he doing?" cried Poppy. Wyatt's head was buried in the bushes. Leaves and berries dropped to the ground.

"Searching for plant pixies," said Sasha.

"For what?" Poppy usually knew everything, but she had never heard of plant pixies.

"Plant pixies are little fairy creatures who live in plants," said Sasha.

"How cute!" exclaimed Poppy.

"Not so much." Wyatt lifted his head. "These pixies may be tiny, but they can hurt a flying horse."

"Can I see a plant pixie?" asked Poppy.

"They're not here. He made the noise," Wyatt said, pointing to a chipmunk. The chipmunk shrugged, then grabbed a berry.

"Happy days!" A purple horse cantered out of the shadows. The tiny braids in her tail twirled as she ran.

Poppy's brown eyes grew wide. She had never seen a purple horse! Her coat was chestnut-brown and so was Wyatt's. Sasha was pale gray with a white patch on her back. All the horses in Verdant Valley were brown, white, black, or gray.

"Who are you?" Poppy asked.

"Kimani is my new friend. She lives in Crystal Cove with the other flying horses. She flies, too," said Sasha.

Kimani opened her wings. Her feathers were deep violet.

Poppy wasn't sure what was more amazing—that her little sister had found other horses with wings or that the flying horses were so beautiful.

Kimani inspected Poppy's mane and tail. "Wow! I never knew regular horses were so glamorous. Can you put pretty flowers in my mane, too?"

"Sure!" Poppy smiled. Sasha wouldn't stand still when Poppy tried to decorate her mane. She turned to Sasha. "I like your new friend."

"Here comes your mom and Caleb." Wyatt pointed across the meadow.

Caleb, their teacher, was old and moved very slowly. Sasha knew it would be a while before they both reached her. She listened to Poppy and Kimani talk about using honeysuckle petals to make their manes smell nice.

"Boring!" Sasha spotted an apple on the ground. "Think fast!" she called to Wyatt.

She kicked the apple with her hoof. It sailed through the air toward him. Wyatt headed the apple back to her. She blocked it with one of her hind legs and knocked it back at him.

Then Wyatt kicked it too hard. The apple rolled under a large white mushroom nearby. Sasha bent to look for it.

A tiny, pointy face peered out at her from under the mushroom.

A plant pixie!

Alexa Pearl is the author of more than forty children's books. She lives in New Jersey with her family.

Paco Sordo is a comics artist, animator, and illustrator based in Spain. Visit him online at pacosordo.com.